TEACHERS RESOURCE GUIDE

JULES VERNE

6470C

First published SADDLEBACK PUBLISHING, INC.
Three Watson Irvine, CA 92618-2767

Published under licence 2006 by R.I.C. PUBLICATIONS® PTY LTD
PO Box 332 Greenwood 6924 Western Australia
www.ricpublications.com.au

Distributed by:
Australasia
R.I.C. Publications, PO Box 332, Greenwood 6924, Western Australia: www.ricpublications.com.au
United Kingdom and Republic of Ireland
Prim-Ed Publishing, Bosheen, New Ross, Co. Wexford, Ireland: www.prim-ed.com
Asia
R.I.C. Publications, 5th Floor, Gotanda Mikado Building, 2-5-8 Hiratsuka, Shinagawa-Ku Tokyo, Japan 142-0051:
www.ricpublications.com

ISBN 978-1-84654-150-6

CONTENTS

TEACHERS NOTES

The novels

The *Classics* series was expressly designed to help pupils with limited reading ability gain access to some of the world's greatest literature. While retaining the essence and stylistic 'flavour' of the original, each of the *Classics* has been expertly adapted to a reading level that never exceeds a reading age of nine years.

A perfect introduction to later, more in-depth investigations of the original works, the *Classics* series utilises a number of strategies to ensure the involvement of reluctant readers: airy, uncomplicated page design; shortened sentences; easy-reading type style; elimination of archaic words and spellings; shortened total book length and handsome illustrations.

The study guides

The *Classics teacher's resource and study guides* provide a wealth of reproducible support materials to help extend the pupils' learning experience. Features include critical background notes on both the author and the era the book was written/set, character descriptions, chapter summaries and eight 'universal' exercises—focusing on plot, theme, character, vocabulary, important literary terms and book report structure. All may be used to follow up the reading of any *Classics* novel.

In addition to the universal exercises, 26 title-specific exercises are included to review, test or enrich the pupil's grasp of important vocabulary and concepts. These enjoyable worksheets, all reproducible, are designed to be used chapter-by-chapter as the pupil's reading of the novel proceeds. At least two exercises are provided for each chapter. One of the two always focuses on key vocabulary. The other may be a simple comprehension check or present an important literary concept such as character analysis, point of view, inference or figurative language. A two-page final exam is also included in every *Classics teacher's resource and study guide*.

Using the study guides

Before assigning any of the reproducible exercises, be sure your pupils each have a personal copy of the glossary and the 'Facts about the author' and the 'Facts about the times' sections. Pupils will need to be familiar with many of the literary terms in order to complete the worksheets. The 'Facts about the author' and 'Facts about the times' lend themselves to any number of writing, art or research projects you may wish to assign.

The title-specific exercises may be used as a springboard for class discussions or role-playing. Alternatively, you may wish to assign some exercises as homework and others as in-class work during the closing minutes of a class period.

All exercises in this guide are designed to accommodate independent study as well as group work. The occasional assignment of study partners or competitive teams often enhances interest and promotes creativity.

FACTS ABOUT THE AUTHOR

Jules Verne
(1828–1905)

The son of a prosperous lawyer, Jules Verne was born in the port of Nantes, France. As a teenager, he moved to Paris, where he, too, studied law. There, his uncle introduced him to popular French writers such as Alexandre Dumas, the author of *The three musketeers*.

That inspired the then young Verne; at the age of 22, he published a one-act comedy called *The broken straws*. While studying for his law degree, Verne became an enthusiastic fan of Edgar Allan Poe's eerie stories, which had recently been translated into French.

Inspired by Poe's imagination, Verne kept on writing. His early work shows a fascination with scientific progress and inventions that would last all his life. Before long, Verne's novels, written for young people as well as adults, became popular throughout the world. His fantastic plots carried his readers all over the Earth, under it and above it.

In time, his works became recognised as unbelievably prophetic. In *20 000 leagues under the sea*, for example, his submarine, *Nautilus*, predated the real powered submarine by 25 years and his spaceship in *From the Earth to the moon* predicted the actual development of such a craft by 100 years.

Today, Verne is regarded (along with H G Wells) as the founding father of science fiction. His best-known novels are *Journey to the centre of the Earth*, *Around the world in 80 days*, *The mysterious island* and *20 000 leagues under the sea*.

For more than 40 years, Jules Verne published at least one book a year. In addition to novels, he wrote short stories, essays, plays, geographical works and even opera librettos.

Jules Verne died at the age of 77 in Amiens, France.

FACTS ABOUT THE TIMES

In 1828, when Jules Verne was born:

Alexandre Dumas published *The three musketeers;* Noah Webster published *The American dictionary of the English language;* Jean Henri Dunant, the founder of the Red Cross, was born; the Austrian composer Franz Schubert died.

In 1870, when *20 000 leagues under the sea* was published:

The novelist Charles Dickens died; France declared war on Prussia; Vladimir Lenin is born.

In 1905, when Jules Verne died:

The play *The Scarlet Pimpernel* opens for the first time; Albert Einstein formulated the theory of special relativity; the first neon light signs appeared; the first movie theatre in America was established in Pittsburgh; Picasso arrived in Paris.

FACTS ABOUT THE CHARACTERS

Phileas Fogg

An unusually calm, precise and daring English gentleman who makes an amazing wager

Jean Passepartout

Fogg's newly hired French servant; a jack-of-all-trades whose many talents serve his master well

Flanagan, Stuart, Sullivan, Fallentin and Ralph

Fogg's friends and fellow card players at the Reform Club

Mr Fix

A determined detective who makes it his business to trail Fogg around the world in the hope of making an arrest

Sir Francis Cromarty

An English gentleman who accidentally gets involved in Fogg's adventures in India

Aouda

A beautiful young Indian woman, who, after being rescued by Fogg and Passepartout, accompanies them on their trip around the world

Judge Obadiah

An Indian magistrate who sentences Fogg and Passepartout to a prison term in Benares

John Bunsby

Captain of a pilot boat that carries the travellers from Hong Kong to Yokohama, Japan

Mr Batulcar

Manager of a troupe of Japanese acrobats

Colonel Stamp Proctor

A burly American who first challenges Fogg to a fist fight and then to a duel

Mudge

Operator of a strange, wind-propelled sled that carries the travellers from Fort Kearny to Omaha, Nebraska

Captain Andrew Speedy

Owner of *Henrietta*, a ship Fogg commandeers to take them from New York City to Ireland

CHAPTER SUMMARIES

Chapter 1

Phileas Fogg, a wealthy and very precise British gentleman, hires a versatile young Frenchman named Jean Passepartout as his personal servant. Shortly after that, Fogg goes, as usual, to spend the evening playing cards at the Reform Club. Fogg and his whist partners discuss the recent robbery of 55 000 pounds from the Bank of England. One man suggests that the robber will escape, while another claims escape is easier than it used to be because 'a man can now go around the world 100 times faster than he could 100 years ago'. Fogg insists that it's possible to travel around the world in 80 days—a statement that is challenged by all the other card players. One of the players, Stuart, bets Fogg 4000 pounds that it can't be done. As the chapter concludes, Fogg says he can and will accomplish this feat if each of his other doubting friends will also bet 4000 pounds. If he loses, Fogg goes on, he will pay them 20 000 pounds. The deal is struck and Fogg declares that he will leave that very evening. It is 2 October 1872.

Chapter 2

Back at his home, Fogg instructs Passepartout to pack two small bags, and the two men quickly board a train for Paris. From Paris, they sail to Suez, Egypt, on a ship named *Mongolia*. Little do they know that, after just a week away, London police have begun speculating that Fogg himself may be the robber since his portrait matches the robber's description. An English detective called Mr Fix is waiting for them when they arrive in Egypt. Without revealing his identity, he discovers that Fogg is bound for Bombay, India, on the next ship out. Eager to make an arrest, Fix arranges to be a passenger on the same ship. He plans to apprehend his prey as soon as Fogg sets foot on English ground in India.

Chapter 3

Rough weather on their journey does not bother Fogg one bit. Fix continues to extract bits of information from Passepartout about his master. In Bombay, Passepartout goes sightseeing and Fix is disappointed that the arrest warrant he needs has not arrived. Unfortunately, Passepartout is furiously attacked by three priests for entering a sacred pagoda without taking off his shoes. The servant fights off his attackers, but only after they've taken his shoes. Shoeless, he meets Fogg at the train station, where they depart for Calcutta. On the train, they meet Sir Francis Cromarty, one of Fogg's whist partners on *Mongolia*. When their trip is halted by a gap in the railway, Fogg buys an elephant and hires a guide to take them to the next station. Along the way they witness preparations for a *suttee*, the ceremonial burning of a man's wife along with the corpse of her husband, a rajah. Fogg suggests they rescue her.

Chapter 4

The guide tells Fogg, Passepartout and Sir Francis that the wife about to be sacrificed is a beautiful young woman named Aouda. Their first try at saving Aouda—reaching her by removing bricks from the pagoda where she is being kept—fails. Calm and collected, Fogg insists that they wait for another chance, which occurs the next morning. A noisy crowd has gathered for the ritual burning—when the dead rajah begins to move! Terrified, the Indians throw themselves on the ground while Passepartout, disguised as the rajah, carries Aouda to the elephant. They quickly escape into the woods, finally reaching the train that will take them to Calcutta. In gratitude, Fogg gives the elephant to the guide. Sir Francis departs to rejoin his troops. Fogg offers to take Aouda to Hong Kong, since she will no longer be safe in India. Fogg and Passepartout, however, are arrested at the train station in Calcutta. Why? They're advised that Passepartout committed a crime when he entered the pagoda wearing his shoes.

Chapter 5

Fix is sitting in the courtroom when Fogg and his servant are sentenced. Once again, the detective has been foiled by the failure of the arrest warrant to arrive! Fogg pays their bail and they immediately sail for Hong Kong on a boat named *Rangoon*. Fix, of course, goes right along with them. Bad weather slows the voyage and *Rangoon* arrives in Hong Kong 24 hours late. When Aouda finds that her cousin in Hong Kong moved away two years ago, Fogg invites her to join them on their trip around the world. Hearing that Fogg plans to go to Japan and then on to America, Fix is desperate. He tells Passepartout the truth about his mission and offers to share the reward if the servant will secretly help him. When Passepartout refuses, Fix gets him drunk so he will miss the boat to Japan. In a strange turn of events,

it is Fogg and Aouda who miss the boat. Instead, they hire a small pilot boat to take them to Japan. As Passepartout is still lying unconscious on the tavern floor, Fix joins them on the pilot boat.

Chapter 6

Captain John Bunsby guides the pilot boat through a typhoon, which is followed by a deadly calm that causes a long delay in Fogg's schedule. They signal an American ship, board her and arrive in Yokohama on 14 November. In the meantime, Passepartout had been carried to *Carnatic*. Thus, he has arrived in Yokohama before Fogg. Penniless, he takes a job as an acrobat in a show. Seeing Fogg and Aouda in the audience, Passepartout leaps out of the 'human pyramid'—causing it to collapse—and joyfully rejoins his master. They soon board a ship bound for San Francisco. Passepartout sees that Fix is also aboard and angrily pounds him with his fists. Fix agrees to stop causing trouble. The ship arrives in San Francisco on 3 December.

Chapter 7

In San Francisco, Fogg, Aouda and Fix happen upon a wild political rally as they're taking a walk. Fogg and an American named Colonel Stamp Proctor, who almost have a fist fight, have an unpleasant exchange of words. On the train to New York, Aouda is upset to see that Colonel Proctor is also a passenger. She asks Fix and Passepartout to keep the two enemies apart. They do this by getting Fogg involved in a game of whist. The engineer stops the train when he determines that an upcoming bridge is unsafe. Several suggestions are made about how to proceed. Finally, it's decided to take the train over the bridge at a very high speed; this succeeds—but the bridge collapses just afterward!

Chapter 8

Colonel Proctor interrupts Fogg's card game as the train trip across the country continues. He challenges Fogg to a duel, which is just about to begin when the train is attacked by a band of Sioux Indians. The engineer is knocked out, and as he falls the throttle is pushed forward. The train speeds ahead at a dangerous rate; no-one knows how to stop it. But Passepartout saves the day again by crawling under the train and separating the out-of-control engine from the cars. When the train of cars stops at Fort Kearny, they realise that three travellers have been taken prisoner by the Sioux. One of their captives is Passepartout! Fix stays behind with Aouda as Fogg leads some soldiers on a rescue mission. Aouda waits and worries all night, but Fogg returns, along with the captives, the next morning. For further transport— because the train has gone on without them—they hire a strange sled with a mast and sails to reach Omaha. From there, they take a train to Chicago and then another to New York. They arrive less than an hour after their ship for Liverpool has departed.

Chapter 9

In New York, Fogg finds a trading ship, *Henrietta*, which is bound for France. Once on board, he locks the captain in his cabin and bribes the sailors to take the ship to England. When they run low on coal, Fogg buys the ship and burns the cabins, bunks and masts as fuel. On 20 December, they land in Ireland and catch a ship bound for Liverpool. But Fix arrests Fogg as soon as they get to England. Fogg is released from prison only a few hours later when the true robber is arrested. The train from Liverpool to London arrives five minutes late; it appears that Fogg has lost his bet!

Chapter 10

Upon arriving at his house in London, Fogg shuts himself in his room, depressed about losing his bet. When he finally comes out, Aouda tries to comfort him. She declares her love and he responds in kind. Fogg sends Passepartout to see Reverend Wilson to arrange their wedding for the next day. Passepartout returns, wildly excited to report that the next day is Sunday; Fogg has miscalculated his return by one day! Meanwhile, Fogg's friends at the Reform Club are nervously waiting. He arrives at exactly a quarter to nine; he's won his bet! Fogg feels satisfied that his hectic trip has resulted in the gain of a charming woman who 'makes him the happiest of men'.

LITERARY GLOSSARY

action what happens in a story; the acts or events that take place

> The war story was full of battle action.

author the writer of a book, story, article etc.

> A B 'Banjo' Paterson was an Australian author.

author's purpose the author's specific goal or reason for writing a certain book

> In that novel, the author's purpose was to make readers laugh.

character a fictional person who plays a part in a story or novel

> Long John Silver is an important character in *Treasure island*.

classic excellent artwork, novel, painting, symphony etc. that remains popular over many years

> Emily Bronte's *Wuthering Heights* is a literary classic.

climax the outcome of the novel's main conflict

> The capture of the criminal was the climax of the detective story.

conflict the struggle between characters or forces at the centre of the story

> The conflict was resolved when the suspect confessed.

description the parts of a story or novel that tell about the appearance of the setting or characters

> Her description of the Alps was breathtaking.

dialogue words spoken by the characters in a novel, story or play

> The dialogue in that comedy is very witty and amusing.

effect in literature, an impression created by the writer

> Murder mysteries often create a suspenseful, chilling effect.

event a specific occurrence; something that happens

> A plane crash is the first event in that adventure novel.

fiction a literary work in which the plot and characters are the products of the author's imagination

> Mary Shelley's *Frankenstein* is a popular work of fiction.

imagery figures of speech that help the reader to visualise the characters or setting; pictures in words

> In Stephen Crane's imagery, the colour of blood suggests courage.

introduction a short section of text that presents and explains a novel; sometimes the first part of a novel that sets the scene

> The introduction to *Frankenstein* is in the form of a letter.

mood the overall feeling or atmosphere the author creates in a story or novel

> The author's skilful use of language created a dismal, hopeless mood.

moral the instructive point of a story or novel; the lesson to be drawn by the reader

> The moral of the story is to choose your friends carefully.

motive the driving force, either internal or external, that makes a character do something

> What was the character's motive for lying?

narrator, narration the character who tells the story in his or her own words; the telling of a story's events

> Jim Hawkins is both the narrator of and a character in *Treasure island*.

novel a long form of fictional literature with a complex plot

> *Emma* is one of the greatest British novels.

pace the speed at which a story or novel develops and moves along

> The pace of the rescue scene was very fast and exciting.

passage a section of a written work; may include just one line or several paragraphs

> My favourite passage described the character's childhood.

plot the chain of events in a story that leads to its outcome

> The war novel's plot is packed with action.

point of view the mental position from which a character sees the events of the story unfold

> The character's great wealth influenced his point of view about the poor.

quotation a passage quoted; the exact words spoken by a character; the words set between quotation marks

> 'It was a season of hope. It was a season of despair', is a famous quotation from *A tale of two cities*.

realism the author's emphasis on showing life as it really is, not romanticised or idealised

> Stephen Crane used great realism in describing the sights and sounds of battle.

sequence the order in which events take place

> To solve the crime, the detective must determine the exact sequence of events.

setting where and when a story happens; the location and time

> The setting of *A Christmas carol* is London in the mid-1800s.

style the special way a writer uses language to express both literary form and his or her own life experience

> Ernest Hemingway's style is famous for his use of short sentences and easy-to-understand words.

symbol a person or thing that stands for, or represents, something else

> In Hawthorne's famous novel, the scarlet letter is a symbol for adultery.

theme the central meaning of a story, play or novel; the main idea, the point

> Ambition and revenge are common themes in Shakespeare's plays.

tone the feeling given by the author's voice; the attitude expressed by the author's use of language

> Is the tone of her dialogue humorous or formal?

voice the author's unique way of telling a story; a combination of personality and use of literary tools; the quality that sets one writer apart from other writers

> Roald Dahl's colourful voice is not hard to recognise.

Name: _____

Date: _____

A Complete the crossword puzzle with words from Chapter 1.

Across

3. not expected or considered before it happens

6. having well-developed muscles

7. tasks that are part of a person's work

8. college teacher of the highest rank

Down

1. the road or course travelled

2. willing to share; not stingy

3. common; normal; most often seen, heard, used etc.

4. parts of the face, such as nose, eyes, chin etc.

5. short in length; not lasting very long

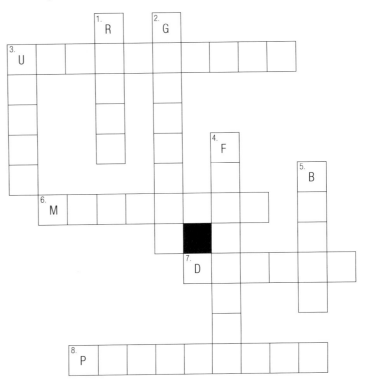

B Use words from the puzzle to complete the sentences.

1. According to Phileas Fogg, 'the _____ does not exist', due to his careful planning.

2. Passepartout was expected to perform his _____ at exact times.

3. Passepartout had a _____ body and a pleasant face.

4. Before going to his club, Fogg had a _____ talk with his new servant.

5. Passepartout had been a fireman and a _____ of gymnastics.

6. Phileas Fogg was known to be rich and often _____.

7. At the Reform Club, Fogg ate breakfast at his _____ table.

8. Fogg went places by the shortest _____ so he wouldn't have to take an extra step.

9. Passepartout noticed that Fogg's _____ were fine and handsome.

Name: _____

Date: _____

Circle a letter to answer each question.

1. About how many years ago does this story take place?

    (a) 75 years

    (b) 140 years

    (c) 100 years

2. In French, what does passepartout mean?

    (a) 'jack-of-all-trades'

    (b) 'trusted servant'

    (c) 'go everywhere'

3. Why did Phileas Fogg avoid most people's company?

    (a) He didn't want to waste time.

    (b) He was a very shy man.

    (c) He was leading a secret life.

4. How much had been stolen from the Bank of England?

    (a) 55 000 dollars

    (b) 55 000 pounds

    (c) 55 000 gold coins

5. What words did the newspapers use to describe the thief?

    (a) 'smooth talking'

    (b) 'very handsome'

    (c) 'well-dressed'

6. Who said, 'I'll bet you four thousand pounds that such a trip is impossible!'?

    (a) Stuart

    (b) Passepartout

    (c) Fallentin

7. Who said, 'You'd lose it all if a single accident made you late!'?

    (a) Ralph

    (b) Flanagan

    (c) Sullivan

8. Who said, 'The robber will have to be very clever to slip through'?

    (a) Fallentin

    (b) Ralph

    (c) Stuart

9. What was the first stop on Fogg's journey?

    (a) Paris

    (b) Liverpool

    (c) Dover

A Circle the hidden words. They may go up, down, forwards, backwards or diagonally. Tick off each word as you find it.

A	S	O	D	E	R	O	L	P	X	E	D
H	A	B	I	T	S	E	S	A	Z	E	E
P	S	E	I	T	U	D	C	O	L	D	V
C	V	D	R	N	K	C	L	B	W	S	I
K	O	L	A	W	E	M	A	S	T	E	R
P	J	N	I	P	F	N	G	E	H	L	R
C	E	O	T	P	O	U	D	R	S	N	A
V	S	R	D	I	C	L	E	V	E	R	M
B	E	O	H	A	N	Q	W	E	D	J	H
M	S	S	D	A	B	U	C	D	E	M	L
L	A	F	J	H	P	Y	E	K	C	P	A
F	N	E	C	E	S	S	A	R	Y	N	B

_____ MASTER   _____ ACCEPT

_____ HABITS   _____ CONTINUE

_____ DUTIES   _____ OBSERVED

_____ NECESSARY   _____ EXPLORED

_____ ARRIVED   _____ PERHAPS

_____ FASHIONABLE   _____ CLEVER

B Use a puzzle word to complete each pair of *synonyms* (words with the same or similar meanings) or *antonyms* (words with opposite meanings).

SYNONYMS

1. maybe / _____

2. routines / _____

3. investigated / _____

4. watched / _____

5. tasks / _____

6. intelligent / _____

ANTONYMS

7. departed / _____

8. servant / _____

9. optional / _____

10. reject / _____

11. terminate / _____

12. outdated / _____

C Use words of your own to complete the pairs below.

SYNONYMS

1. thief / _____

2. brief / _____

ANTONYMS

3. usually / _____

4. generous / _____

A Circle the hidden words. They may go up, down, forwards, backwards or diagonally. Tick off each word as you find it.

_____ NAKED	_____ DESPAIR
_____ SCENT	_____ HURTLED
_____ VISA	_____ DETECTIVE
_____ ANCHOR	_____ WARRANT
_____ RASCAL	_____ OVERCOME
_____ SIGHTSEEING	_____ PASSPORT

H	A	W	E	V	I	T	C	E	T	E	D
K	U	L	O	C	X	A	T	S	T	Y	Y
A	E	R	B	N	T	S	R	M	L	K	T
N	U	P	T	A	Q	I	O	D	F	N	W
C	F	H	G	L	E	V	P	B	E	T	S
H	S	N	A	K	E	D	S	C	L	N	D
O	T	C	I	R	Z	D	S	K	N	A	E
R	A	S	C	A	L	C	A	M	O	R	R
Y	U	O	L	D	E	S	P	A	I	R	G
I	M	A	W	S	D	R	T	H	J	A	Y
E	J	C	R	Y	Y	P	L	M	D	W	H
S	I	G	H	T	S	E	E	I	N	G	I

B Write an *antonym* (word with the opposite meaning) from the box next to each word from Chapter 2. (Hint: You will *not* use all the words in the box.)

gigantic	little	fail	shouted	deceitful
despised	agreed	fake	departed	trustworthy

1. genuine / _____
2. succeed / _____
3. popular / _____
4. honest / _____

5. objected / _____
6. muttered / _____
7. enormous / _____
8. remained / _____

C The words below are *synonyms* (words with the same or similar meanings) of words in Part A. Unscramble the words to complete each pair.

1. scamp / **sarlac**

2. bare / **daken**

3. aroma / **nesct**

4. hopelessness / **erapids**

Name: _____

Date: _____

A Read the *causes* on the left. Then write a letter to match each *cause* with its *effect* on the right.

1. ____ The servant gets 10 minutes to prepare for a round-the-world trip.

2. ____ A beggar woman reaches out to Phileas Fogg.

3. ____ Passepartout leaves the gaslight on in his room.

4. ____ Word of Fogg's trip spreads around London.

5. ____ London police suspect Fogg of robbing the bank.

6. ____ Passepartout asks Fix for directions to the passport office.

7. ____ Passepartout packs only a small bag for their trip.

8. ____ Passepartout reveals that Bombay is their next stop.

(a) Fogg says that he'll have to pay for it.

(b) He shops in Egypt for shirts and shoes.

(c) Mr Fix meets the ship, *Mongolia*, in Egypt.

(d) He thinks his master is joking.

(e) People place bets on whether or not he'll succeed.

(f) Fix requests that an arrest warrant be sent to Bombay.

(g) The detective begs the consul *not* to stamp Fogg's passport.

(h) He gives her the money he'd won playing whist.

B In your own words, explain the *effect* of each *cause* below.

1. *cause:* Passepartout tells Fix his master is carrying a fortune in new bank notes.

   effect: _____

   _____

2. *cause:* Passepartout lets Fix see his master's passport.

   effect: _____

   _____

3. *cause:* Many people notice that the description of the robber matches Phileas Fogg's portrait.

   effect: _____

   _____

Name: _____

Date: _____

A Circle the hidden words. They may go up, down, forwards, backwards or diagonally. Tick off each word as you find it.

_____ GAP   _____ ERRAND

_____ DELAY   _____ FORBIDDEN

_____ AGILE   _____ CONFIDED

_____ PAGODA   _____ EXTERIOR

_____ SACRED   _____ FESTIVAL

_____ QUARRY   _____ CONDUCTOR

A	G	I	L	E	H	P	T	V	B	P	W
O	M	B	C	F	P	D	E	R	C	A	S
F	G	D	E	C	M	E	K	S	E	G	E
L	O	F	X	O	P	L	L	I	Q	A	R
E	H	R	C	N	J	A	G	F	U	P	O
R	S	A	B	F	V	Y	V	H	A	E	I
R	D	C	O	I	Y	H	L	G	R	J	R
A	M	D	T	D	K	O	I	R	N	E
N	O	S	A	E	F	D	C	P	Y	A	T
D	E	P	S	D	A	O	E	L	R	D	X
F	A	R	O	T	C	U	D	N	O	C	E

B Write a word from the puzzle under the definition that matches it.

1. an Asian tower with several stories

_____

2. nimble; able to move with ease

_____

3. prohibited; not done or allowed

_____

4. one who collects fares on a train

_____

5. holiday; time of feasting or celebrating

_____

6. one who's being chased or hunted

_____

7. told someone a secret

_____

8. an opening, blank or empty space

_____

9. holy; deserving of the greatest respect

_____

10. a short trip to accomplish something

_____

Name: _____

Date: _____

First, complete the sentences with words from the box. Then number the events to show which happened first, second and so on. (Hint: You will *not* use all the words in the box.)

lost	rescue	priests	pagoda	conductor
ship	gained	captain	sacrifice	dangerous
train	rabbit	burned	carriage	ceremonies
rajah	errand	curious	elephant	transportation

1. Fogg and Sir Francis search for _____ to Allahabad.   ☐

2. Cromarty explains that a suttee is a human _____.   ☐

3. Reaching Bombay, Fogg calculates that he has _____ two days.   ☐

4. Fix suggests that Fogg's trip hides a secret _____.   ☐

5. The _____ explains that there's an 80-kilometre gap in the railway.   ☐

6. Passepartout visits a splendid _____ on Malebar Hill.   ☐

7. Fogg suspects that the dish he's served for dinner isn't really _____.   ☐

8. Hearing voices coming, the guide hides the _____ in the trees.   ☐

9. Fix tells Passepartout that India is a _____ place.   ☐

10. Fogg, Passepartout and Fix board a _____ for Calcutta.   ☐

11. Fogg suggests they _____ the young woman.   ☐

12. They see guards carrying the corpse of a _____.   ☐

13. Three angry _____ beat Passepartout and remove his shoes.   ☐

Name: _____

Date: _____

 A Complete the crossword puzzle with words from Chapter 4.

Across

3. solemnly promised

4. bold and dangerous

6. dazed condition in which a person can barely think or act

7. a shadowy form, supposedly the spirit of a dead person

8. thankfulness

Down

1. one who buys or sells goods for profit

2. inmates; those taken captive

5. young person with no parents

9. unfriendly; cold in feeling

B Use words from the puzzle to complete the sentences.

1. Aouda was the daughter of a wealthy _____.

2. The fumes from the fire left Aouda in a _____.

3. The guide's eyes glistened with _____ when Fogg gave him the elephant.

4. Fogg knew that trying to save Aouda would be very _____.

5. The _____ had to appear before Judge Obadiah.

6. Fogg's exterior was _____, but his heart was warm.

7. After being left an _____, Aouda was married to the old rajah.

8. Sir Francis _____ to help Fogg rescue the beautiful young woman.

9. Clouds of smoke made Passepartout look like a _____.

Circle a letter to complete the sentence or answer the question.

1. The guide told Fogg that Aouda had been

   (a) educated in Bombay.

   (b) left an orphan.

   (c) both a and b.

2. The rajah's relatives believed that Aouda

   (a) had stolen the rajah's money.

   (b) should die by his side.

   (c) deserved to be rewarded.

3. Why did the Indians cry out in terror and throw themselves to the ground?

   (a) Clouds had suddenly appeared.

   (b) The pagoda's door opened.

   (c) They saw that the rajah was moving.

4. The ghostly figure that looked like the rajah was really

   (a) Aouda.

   (b) Passepartout.

   (c) Phileas Fogg.

5. In return for the guide's help, Fogg gave him

   (a) 4000 pounds.

   (b) a gold watch.

   (c) the elephant.

6. Imagine Aouda's surprise to wake up in a train

   (a) accompanied by three strangers.

   (b) still married to the rajah.

   (c) dressed in new clothing.

7. Phileas Fogg offered to take Aouda

   (a) on his trip around the world.

   (b) to her cousin in Hong Kong.

   (c) back to the pagoda.

8. Why did Sir Francis get off the train at Benares?

   (a) He left to join his troops.

   (b) He was tired of travelling.

   (c) His family lived there.

9. Who was waiting for Fogg, Aouda and Passepartout at the train station in Calcutta?

   (a) Mr Fix

   (b) Judge Obadiah

   (c) a policeman

Name: _____

Date: _____

Think about the events that occurred in Chapter 4. If you need help to answer the questions, look back through the chapter.

1. Why did Fogg wonder if the guide might side with the Indians instead of the rescuers?

   _____

   _____

2. Why did Fogg suggest waiting until night before going after Aouda?

   _____

   _____

3. Why did Fogg think it would be wise to take Aouda to Hong Kong?

   _____

   _____

4. Something happened that made Sir Francis 'shake his fists' and the guide 'gnash his teeth'. What had happened?

   _____

   _____

5. Why did the Indians lay the beautiful young woman next to her dead husband?

   _____

   _____

6. After the Indians lit the fire, what made them cry out and throw themselves on the ground?

   _____

   _____

7. What tipped Fogg that their trick had been discovered?

   _____

   _____

8. How did Aouda show gratitude to her rescuers?

   _____

   _____

A **Complete the crossword puzzle with words from Chapter 5.**

Across

2. something given in return for good work or a good deed

6. contented feeling when one's needs or wishes are met

7. wild anger; great rage

8. guesses of wrongdoing made with little or no proof

Down

1. headed for; on the way to a destination

3. persons who saw or heard something that happened

4. to have something set aside for yourself or someone else

5. to force yourself or your thoughts on someone without being asked

6. one who watches closely and secretly

(crossword grid with clues: 1. B, 2. R, 3. W, 4. R, 5. I, 6. S, 7. F, 8. S)

B **Use words from the puzzle to complete the sentences.**

1. Fogg asked Passepartout to _____ three rooms on *Carnatic*.

2. Passepartout began to have _____ that Mr Fix might be a _____.

3. Judge Obadiah said, 'These three priests are _____.'

4. Fix knew that *Rangoon* was _____ for Hong Kong.

5. A big _____ was being offered for the capture of the bank robber.

6. Aouda didn't want to _____ on Fogg's trip around the world.

7. A storm at sea knocked *Rangoon* around with _____.

8. As Fogg was sentenced, Fix rubbed his hands in _____.

Circle a letter to answer the question or complete the sentence.

1. What evidence did Judge Obadiah produce as proof that a crime had been committed?

   (a) Fogg's hat

   (b) Passepartout's shoes

   (c) Fix's report

2. Fogg was sentenced to a fine of 150 pounds and

   (a) a week in prison.

   (b) hard labour.

   (c) to make an apology.

3. What ship did Fogg board next and where was it headed?

   (a) *Mongolia*, to Egypt

   (b) *Bombay*, to Australia

   (c) *Rangoon*, to Hong Kong

4. When Fix travelled on with them, Passepartout wondered if the man

   (a) wanted to arrest Fogg.

   (b) worked for Judge Obadiah.

   (c) was a spy for the Reform Club.

5. The departure of *Carnatic* was delayed because

   (a) the seas were too rough.

   (b) its boiler was being repaired.

   (c) Fogg was already 24 hours late.

6. Why did Fogg invite Aouda to join them on their round-the-world journey?

   (a) Her cousin had moved away.

   (b) Passepartout had a crush on her.

   (c) She begged Fogg to take her along.

7. What two surprises awaited Fogg and Aouda at the harbour?

   (a) Fix was drunk and Passepartout had been arrested.

   (b) Passepartout was missing and *Carnatic* had already departed.

   (c) Their luggage was missing and *Carnatic* had sunk.

8. John Busby's pilot boat was headed for

   (a) Shanghai.

   (b) Korea.

   (c) Beijing.

9. What did Fogg do that made Fix feel uncomfortable?

   (a) threatened him with a lawsuit

   (b) sent him to look for Passepartout

   (c) invited Fix to come with them

Name: _____

Date: _____

A Circle the hidden words. They may go up, down, forwards, backwards or diagonally. Tick off each word as you find it.

A	S	F	W	S	T	A	B	O	R	C	A
G	D	H	I	L	C	V	S	X	F	G	P
E	I	Q	M	F	L	H	E	A	R	T	Y
O	M	A	P	O	S	C	V	B	N	M	F
E	A	D	B	N	C	X	T	O	T	P	L
T	R	B	E	D	F	S	A	R	W	R	A
A	Y	S	N	B	I	O	E	P	S	U	O
X	P	P	L	O	K	A	W	I	D	M	O
C	O	P	H	M	S	R	R	T	L	P	B
L	K	P	R	O	G	R	E	S	S	L	M
A	B	E	N	Y	O	H	J	O	M	E	A
N	T	A	V	E	R	N	A	S	P	D	B

____ HOIST   ____ LOBBY

____ TYPHOON   ____ HEARTY

____ TAVERN   ____ BAMBOO

____ PYRAMID   ____ ACROBATS

____ ALLIES   ____ RUMPLED

____ TREASON   ____ PROGRESS

B Use words from the puzzle to complete the sentences.

1. The pilot boat made good _____ on its voyage to Shanghai.

2. The _____ of performers fell like a house of cards!

3. _____ jumped from the tip of one long nose to another.

4. Passepartout said that he and Fix were not friends, but _____.

5. During the _____, rain hit the boat like bullets.

6. Batulcar stopped Fogg, Aouda and Passepartout in the theatre _____.

7. Fix was rather _____ after Passepartout had furiously attacked him with his fists.

8. Fogg told Bunsby to _____ the pilot boat's flag.

Name: _____

Date: _____

First, complete the sentences with words from the box. Then number the events to show which happened first, second and so on. (Hint: You will *not* use all the words.)

acrobat	calm	Fogg	Tokyo	audience
typhoon	neck	friends	Bunsby	Shanghai
bullets	roof	clown	servant	Yokohama
cannon	hair	Aouda	pyramid	San Francisco

1. Passepartout agrees to be part of the human _____. ☐

2. The boat slows down when the wind becomes too _____. ☐

3. Mr Fix asks Passepartout if they can be _____. ☐

4. Passepartout arrives in _____ without a penny in his pocket. ☐

5. Mr Fix offers to pay _____ for his share of the trip. ☐

6. Passepartout dashes into the _____ to greet Fogg. ☐

7. When the _____ hits, the pilot boat begins to shake and roll. ☐

8. As the pyramid slowly rises to the _____, the audience applauds. ☐

9. Fogg, Aouda and Passepartout board a ship bound for _____. ☐

10. Passepartout grabs Fix's _____ and begins to punch him. ☐

11. Bunsby uses a flag and a _____ to signal the American ship. ☐

12. Passepartout follows a _____ to a theatre. ☐

13. Batulcar says that he has no use for a _____. ☐

Name: _____

Date: _____

A Think about how the characters behaved in Chapter 6. Circle two words that describe each character's attitudes and actions.

1.	Phileas Fogg	cowardly	generous	bold	despicable
2.	Mr Fix	forthright	secretive	determined	lazy
3.	Passepartout	acrobatic	pathetic	mystified	apologetic
4.	Aouda	grateful	enthusiastic	aggressive	spiteful

B Write a character's name next to his or her line of dialogue.

1. [_____]: 'Hoist your flag!'

2. [_____]: 'I admit I tried to stop him.'

3. [_____]: 'We are allies, perhaps.'

4. [_____]: 'Would you be needing a servant, sir?'

5. [_____]: 'Let us go to the ship, young man.'

C Answer each question with the name of a character *not* mentioned in Part A.

1. Who was afraid of losing his reward of 200 pounds? [_____]

2. Who asked Passepartout if he was a 'pretty strong fellow'? [_____]

3. Who worried that a typhoon was coming? [_____]

4. Whose 'feelings were soothed' when Fogg gave him a handful of pound notes? [_____]

Name: _____

Date: _____

A Complete the crossword puzzle with words from Chapter 7.

Across

4. a part of the river where the water moves very swiftly

6. an object used as a barrier

7. a large group of people who have gathered for a particular purpose

Down

1. to move just a little

2. thought that something would happen; looked forward to it

3. another name for North American bison

4. to turn or go backward

5. the noisy uproar of many voices

B Choose a *synonym* (word with a same or similar meaning) from the box to replace each word in bold print from Chapter 7. Write it on the line. (Hint: You will *not* use all the words.)

travellers	pistols	problem	hobby	rifles	Indians
engineers	guard	worried	chore	attack	enraged

1. bought some **revolvers**

   _____

2. tried to **protect** Aouda

   _____

3. his favourite **pastime**

   _____

4. some **trouble** ahead

   _____

5. **furious** at the delay

   _____

6. the **passengers** complained

   _____

C Write a letter from the box on the right to match each word in bold print from Chapter 7 with its *antonym* (word with the opposite meaning).

1. _____ creek was **swollen**

2. _____ money was **useless**

3. _____ **arrived** in the city

4. _____ the **last** buffalo

(a) departed

(b) shrunken

(c) first

(d) helpful

A Read the *causes* on the left. Then write a letter to match each *cause* with its *effect* on the right.

1. _____ The next train to New York will not leave until 6.00 pm.

2. _____ Passepartout hears tales of Indians attacking trains.

3. _____ At Green River, Colonel Proctor boards the train.

4. _____ A big, red-bearded fellow tries to hit Fogg.

5. _____ The train stops abruptly.

6. _____ The bridge just ahead appears to be unsafe.

7. _____ A herd of buffalo block the train track.

8. _____ The train full of passengers crosses the bridge at high speed.

(a) Fix steps between them and takes the blow.

(b) Colonel Proctor gets out to investigate.

(c) Aouda becomes alarmed.

(d) The conductor wants passengers to walk to a nearby town.

(e) The bridge collapses as soon as the train passes over.

(f) Fogg, Aouda and Passepartout wait at the International Hotel.

(g) He buys some revolvers.

(h) The train is late reaching Utah.

B In your own words, explain the *effect* of each *cause* below.

1. *cause:* At the rally Fogg and Fix are caught between two warring groups.

   effect: _____

   _____

2. *cause:* Thousands of buffalo stream across the railroad tracks.

   effect: _____

   _____

3. *cause:* Heavy rains had swollen the creek.

   effect: _____

   _____

Name: _____

Date: _____

A Circle the hidden words. They may go up, down, forwards, backwards or diagonally. Tick off each word as you find it.

_____ FORT	_____ WEAPONS
_____ DUEL	_____ DIAMOND
_____ FRANK	_____ HUDDLED
_____ SPADE	_____ INSOLENT
_____ THROTTLE	_____ LANDMARKS
_____ INJURED	_____ UNCONSCIOUS

L	T	H	R	O	T	T	L	E	V	K	W
J	A	H	I	N	J	U	R	E	D	S	E
D	E	N	A	O	P	Z	M	F	U	C	G
I	B	C	D	E	R	T	R	O	F	D	M
A	V	G	I	M	D	P	I	Y	U	A	H
M	S	C	V	N	A	C	R	W	E	U	O
O	E	K	L	O	S	R	N	B	D	C	P
N	F	D	A	N	P	O	K	D	A	E	W
D	R	E	O	G	H	I	L	S	P	R	T
S	A	C	B	W	O	E	A	E	S	P	Y
C	N	F	G	A	D	S	C	O	N	L	Z
U	K	O	S	N	O	P	A	E	W	T	H

B Use words from the puzzle to complete the sentences.

1. Colonel Proctor challenged Phileas Fogg to a _____.

2. In an _____ voice, Proctor suggested that Fogg should play a _____ instead of a _____.

3. The sight of familiar _____ told Mudge that they had reached Omaha, Nebraska.

4. The train hurtled past the station while the engineer was _____.

5. The travellers _____ together in the cold winds.

6. Fogg's face was calm and _____ as he made his request.

7. As the engineer fell, his body pushed the _____ full forward.

8. _____ Kearny was now just two miles away.

A Write T or F to show whether each statement below is *true* or *false*.

1. _____ Bound for New York, the train heads west.

2. _____ Fogg tells Proctor he's in a hurry to return to England.

3. _____ Each man carried two revolvers.

4. _____ The engineer's body pushes the throttle backward.

5. _____ Passepartout attaches the cars to the engine.

6. _____ The soldiers at Fort Kearny frighten off the Sioux.

7. _____ Proctor is taken prisoner by the departing Sioux.

8. _____ Fogg asks the soldiers to help rescue the prisoners.

9. _____ Fogg asks Fix to stay behind and protect Aouda.

10. _____ All night long, Aouda worries about Fogg and Passepartout.

11. _____ Fogg, Passepartout and Aouda continue their journey on the train.

12. _____ In Chicago, they miss the train bound for New York.

B Rewrite the *false* sentences from Part A to make them *true*. (Hint: You should rewrite six sentences.)

1. _____
   _____

2. _____
   _____

3. _____
   _____

4. _____
   _____

5. _____
   _____

6. _____
   _____

Name: _____

Date: _____

A Complete the crossword puzzle with words from Chapter 9.

Across

1. city where a state or country's government is located

4. things that get in the way or block progress

7. something placed as a bet, such as money

8. deeds that show great courage, skill or strength

9. wanting all you can get without thinking of what others need

10. tall poles that support a boat's sails

Down

2. a very short time; a moment

3. continued making an effort

5. paid someone to do something wrong or something he or she didn't want to do

6. rooms on a ship with hanging sleeping berths

B Use words from the puzzle to complete the sentences.

1. First, Fogg had the _____ burned, then the spare deck, the rafts and the

   _____.

2. On 20 December, they reached Dublin, the _____ of Ireland.

3. Having completed his tour of the world, Fogg feared that he had lost his

   _____.

4. At Fogg's offer, _____ Captain Speedy changed his mind in an

   _____.

5. The servant feared that he'd put _____ in his master's path.

6. Passepartout amazed the sailors with his acrobatic _____.

7. Fogg _____ until he finally _____ the crew to
   head for Liverpool.

Name: _____

Date: _____

To complete each statement below, unscramble one word and add one word from the box. (Hint: You will *not* use all the words in the box.)

Carnatic	Bordeaux	sailor	passengers
Henrietta	Liverpool	bribe	Newfoundland
London	station	docks	Captain Speedy

1. The **materes** _____ bound for _____ seemed to be Fogg's best chance of reaching England in time.

2. At the _____, Fogg found a **ginratd** _____ ship that was leaving in an hour.

3. The **nictapa** _____ told Fogg that he never carried _____.

4. Fogg locked _____ in his cabin so he could take **mocnamd** _____ of the ship.

5. The **dryege** _____ sailors were happy to accept Fogg's _____.

6. While passing the coast of _____, **traietHen** _____ weathered a terrible storm.

7. The **nerinege** _____ warned that there was only enough fuel to get to _____, France.

8. Fogg was just six hours from _____ when he was **sterdare** _____.

A Circle the hidden words. They may go up, down, forwards, backwards or diagonally. Tick off each word as you find it.

L	U	F	H	T	I	A	F	D	U	X	M
T	F	B	J	R	L	W	C	A	N	I	T
Q	C	A	V	S	U	S	P	E	N	S	E
N	O	A	Z	B	E	M	L	D	F	V	L
O	Y	R	X	Y	S	K	R	O	L	C	E
B	N	W	U	E	N	A	R	U	M	X	G
L	O	B	R	O	W	T	I	Y	M	B	R
E	M	N	O	T	U	I	L	S	W	Q	A
Z	E	A	S	N	B	U	R	C	O	D	M
E	R	A	E	G	D	U	R	G	C	O	S
V	E	R	N	S	L	S	O	E	V	N	B
U	C	N	E	L	A	N	I	M	I	R	C

_____ BONDS   _____ CEREMONY

_____ MURMUR   _____ CRIMINAL

_____ NOBLE   _____ SUSPENSE

_____ EXACT   _____ FAITHFUL

_____ GRUDGE   _____ EASTWARD

_____ FORTUNE   _____ TELEGRAMS

B Write the word from the puzzle that matches each definition.

1. [_____] : messages sent by a code of electrical signals

2. [_____] : having or showing good character and morals

3. [_____] : accurate; strictly correct; without mistakes

4. [_____] : certificates sold by a business to raise money

5. [_____] : the condition of being anxious and uncertain

6. [_____] : a low, steady sound, such as faraway voices

7. [_____] : a serious act done according to strict rules

8. [_____] : bad feeling against someone who supposedly did wrong

9. [_____] : remaining loyal and constant in fulfilling a responsibility

10. [_____] : in the direction of the east; opposite of westward

First, complete the sentences with words from the box. Then number the events to show which happened first, second and so on. (Hint: You will *not* use all the words.)

door	Sunday	forgiveness	heart	ceremony
gas	cheering	cooperation	friend	Saturday
wife	criminal	gentlemen	reward	relatives
bride	licence	reputation	fortune	detective

1. Fogg divides 1000 pounds between Passepartout and the unlucky

   _____. ☐

2. People waiting outside the Reform Club begin _____. ☐

3. Fogg asks Aouda for her _____. ☐

4. Passepartout is honoured when he's asked to give the _____ away. ☐

5. Passepartout turns off the _____ that's been burning for 80 days. ☐

6. People realise that Fogg is not a _____ when the real robber

   is arrested. ☐

7. Fogg tells Aouda that he no longer has any _____. ☐

8. Fogg offers the cab driver a _____ if he arrives at the Reform

   Club in time. ☐

9. Feeling sad, Passepartout waits outside Fogg's closed _____. ☐

10. Fogg tells Aouda that his _____ belongs to her. ☐

11. Aouda offers to become Fogg's _____. ☐

12. Passepartout reports that tomorrow is _____. ☐

13. Passepartout is sent to arrange a wedding _____. ☐

Draw on your own personal experiences, ideas and opinions to answer the questions. Write on the back of this sheet if you need more room.

1. Believing he's lost his bet, Fogg shuts himself up in his room. This makes Aouda and Passepartout very worried.

   How would you react if someone you cared for was terribly disappointed about something? What could you say or do to help your friend cheer up?

   _____

   _____

2. Until the real robber was caught, people all over England suspected that Fogg had stolen the money.

   Have you or someone you know ever been falsely accused? How did it feel? What did you do about it? Was the real culprit ever identified?

   _____

   _____

3. Fogg's friends at the Reform Club are very anxious about whether or not he'll arrive on time. To calm their nerves, they play a game of cards.

   What do you do to take your mind off your troubles or pass the time while you're waiting? What helps you to 'calm your nerves'?

   _____

   _____

4. Fogg's confusion about the exact day and date almost cost him his bet.

   Have you ever made—or almost made—a mistake that had very serious consequences? Describe what happened.

   _____

   _____

5. Fogg was delighted to find that he'd won his bet after all.

   Tell about a time you won something that mattered to you. Perhaps it was a race or another kind of competition. Describe how you felt.

   _____

   _____

Name: _____

Date: _____

First, complete the sentences with words from the box. Then number the events to show which happened first, second and so on. (Hint: You will not use all the words.)

hours	house	Calcutta	pagoda	discovery
tour	Bombay	seconds	*Henrietta*	*General Grant*
rajah	Chicago	*Carnatic*	reconsider	San Francisco

1. The _____ sails without Fogg, Aouda and Fix. ☐

2. The _____ carries the travellers to San Francisco. ☐

3. Fogg wins his bet by a margin of three _____. ☐

4. Fogg bets that he can _____ the world in 80 days. ☐

5. While visiting the _____, Passepartout is attacked. ☐

6. In Omaha, the travellers board a train for _____. ☐

7. Many Englishmen _____ Fogg's hasty departure. ☐

8. As the suttee ceremony begins, Passepartout pretends to be the

   _____. ☐

9. Fogg pays Captain Speedy a fortune for the _____. ☐

10. Fogg and Passepartout head for _____ when they leave Egypt. ☐

11. In _____, Fogg and Fix accidentally get embroiled in a political rally. ☐

12. Passepartout explores Fogg's _____ from top to bottom. ☐

13. Passepartout makes an amazing _____ when he visits

    Reverend Wilson. ☐

Circle a letter to correctly answer each question or complete each statement.

1. How much did Fogg bet that he could travel around the world in 80 days?

   (a) his expenses only

   (b) 4000 pounds

   (c) 20 000 dollars

   (d) 20 000 pounds

2. How could Fogg's emotional make-up best be described?

   (a) reserved, meek, mild

   (b) expressive, unpredictable, volatile

   (c) composed, unperturbed, remote

   (d) forlorn, withdrawn, melancholy

3. What did Passepartout contribute to the success of Fogg's journey?

   (a) absolute confidentiality

   (b) several daring deeds

   (c) his life savings

   (d) supervision of Aouda

4. Fogg said he didn't believe in the *unforeseen*. But one completely unforeseen outcome of his journey was

   (a) finding a wife.

   (b) fighting a duel.

   (c) losing a day.

   (d) regaining his reputation.

5. Why didn't it matter that the travellers arrived in Hong Kong 24 hours late?

   (a) They were already ahead of schedule.

   (b) The *Rangoon* would depart the next morning.

   (c) Passepartout was nowhere to be found.

   (d) The *Carnatic* wasn't ready to depart.

Answer each question in your own words. Write in complete sentences.

1. Where did Fogg get the idea that a person could travel around the world in 80 days?

   _____

   _____

2. Why was Fix confident that he'd recognise Fogg when he got off the ship in Egypt?

   _____

   _____

3. Describe the ceremony called a *suttee*.

   _____

   _____

4. What offer did Mr Fix make to Passepartout at the tavern in Hong Kong? Did Passepartout accept?

   _____

   _____

5. Why did Fogg burn *Henrietta's* cabins, bunks, masts and railing?

   _____

   _____

6. How did Fogg respond when Mr Fix begged his forgiveness for arresting him?

   _____

   _____

7. At the end of the story, Passepartout saw something that made his face 'glow as brightly as the tropical sun'. What did he see?

   _____

   _____

Title of novel _____

Choose one 'bonus marks' project from each column. Complete the short-term project on the back of this sheet. To complete the second project, follow your teacher's instructions.

Short-term projects

1. Write brief captions for any four illustrations in the book.

2. Draw a picture of your favourite character. Be sure the clothing and hairstyles are appropriate to the times.

3. Write a diary entry for one of the main characters. Describe, from that character's point of view, an important event from the novel.

4. Write a short paragraph explaining why you think the author chose to write about the particular time and place of the novel's setting.

5. Draw a simple map, showing various locations mentioned in the novel.

6. Choose any page from the novel. Rewrite all the dialogue.

7. Playing the role of a newspaper reporter, write a brief article describing one of the events that occur in the novel.

Long-term projects

1. Use a reference book or conduct research on the Internet to find a song that was popular at the time this story takes place. Read or sing it to the class.

2. Write a description of the daily life of ordinary people at the time this story was written. Use library resources to find information.

3. Make a diorama depicting one of the important scenes in the story.

4. Ask a librarian to help you find a recipe for a dish that was popular at the time depicted in the story. Make it for the class.

5. Make a chart showing 'then and now' comparisons between the story's location and people at the time the novel is set and as to what it is like today.

6. Make an audio recording of any two chapters of the novel.

Name: _____

Date: _____

Title of novel _____

Five elements make up a plot: *characters, setting, conflict, climax* and *conclusion*. **Review the glossary definition of each element. Answer the questions about the novel you just read.**

1. What is the **setting** (time and place) of the novel?

   _____

   _____

2. What **conflict** or **conflicts** do the main **characters** face?

   _____

   _____

   _____

3. Explain the **climax** of these conflicts (how they are resolved).

   _____

   _____

   _____

4. Was the outcome of the **plot** surprising? Why or why not?

   _____

   _____

   _____

5. Does the novel focus mostly on **character**, **plot** or **setting**? Explain your answer.

   _____

   _____

   _____

6. What might have been a *different* way for the conflicts to be resolved? Think of some events that would have changed the **conclusion** of the plot. Write your new ending here.

   _____

   _____

   _____

   _____

Name: _____

Date: _____

Title of novel _____

Review the glossary definition of *theme*. Then study the literary themes listed in the box.

bravery	loyalty	revenge	revolution	nature
guilt	love	war	repentance	courage
madness	science	injustice	greed	regret
hope	friendship	youth		

Authors often want to include a message about their themes. This message, usually a deeply-held belief, is expressed in the story.

Think about the novel you just read. What theme or themes can you recognise? What was the main idea? What point was the author trying to make about that theme? What message was delivered?

Choose two or three themes from the box or write your own. Then write a sentence explaining the author's belief about that theme. (This kind of sentence is called a *thematic statement*.)

EXAMPLE: *Romeo and Juliet* by William Shakespeare

Theme: hatred

Thematic statement: Hatred between families can have tragic consequences for innocent individuals.

Theme 1: _____

Thematic statement: _____

_____

_____

Theme 2: _____

Thematic statement: _____

_____

_____

Theme 3: _____

Thematic statement: _____

_____

_____

Name: _____

Date: _____

Title of novel _____

Review the glossary definition of *character*. Name two important characters from the novel you just read. Write a brief description of each.

1. Character: _____

    Description: _____

    _____

2. Character: _____

    Description: _____

    _____

3. Which character did you find most interesting?

    Explain why. _____

    _____

4. Describe the main conflict this character faces.

    _____

    _____

5. How is this conflict finally resolved?

    _____

    _____

6. Does the plot outcome make the character happy?

    Explain how. _____

    _____

    _____

7. Write three lines of dialogue or a description from the novel that helped you understand this character.

    _____

    _____

    _____

8. On the back of this sheet, write a sentence telling how you and the character are **alike**. Then write another sentence telling how the two of you are **different**.

Name: _____

Date: _____

Title of novel _____

Look back through the novel you just read. Find ten words that were new to you. First, list the words on the lines below. Check a dictionary if you're not sure what each word means. Finally, use each word in a sentence of your own.

1. _____   6. _____

2. _____   7. _____

3. _____   8. _____

4. _____   9. _____

5. _____   10. _____

1. _____
_____

2. _____
_____

3. _____
_____

4. _____
_____

5. _____
_____

6. _____
_____

7. _____
_____

8. _____
_____

9. _____
_____

10. _____
_____

Title of novel _____

1. Review the glossary definition of **conflict**. Describe one example of a conflict in this novel.

_____

_____

2. Review the glossary definition of **imagery**. Give two examples of the author's clever use of figurative language.

_____

_____

3. Select your favourite short **passage** from the novel. Write it out.

_____

_____

_____

4. Describe the **setting** of the novel. When and where does the story take place?

_____

_____

5. Review the glossary definition of **motive**. Explain the motive, or driving force, behind the main character's actions.

_____

_____

6. Review the glossary definition of **quotation**. Select a memorable quote from the novel and write it out.

_____

_____

7. Think about a major event in the story. What was the main character's **point of view** about that event? Explain how the author revealed that character's point of view.

_____

_____

_____

Name: _____

Date: _____

Title of novel: _____

Imagine you are a book reviewer for a newspaper. Your job is to describe the novel you just read for your readers. Before you write your review—which will contain both fact and opinion—you must take notes. Use this form to record the information you will use in your article.

> **Book title:** _____
>
> **Author:** _____

1. What was the **author's purpose** in writing this book? (Examples: to amuse, terrify, inform, protest, inspire) Name more than one purpose, if appropriate.

   _____

2. What **type** of novel is this? (Examples: adventure, fantasy, comedy, tragedy, mystery, action, drama) Name more than one type, if appropriate.

   _____

3. Describe the **main character** in two or three sentences. Use meaningful details.

   _____

   _____

   _____

   _____

4. Describe two or three **supporting characters**. Explain each character's relationship to the main character.

   _____

   _____

   _____

   _____

5. Write one or two sentences from the novel as examples of powerful **description**. (Hint: Look for vivid sights, sounds, smells or feelings.)

   _____

   _____

   _____

   _____

6.   Write one or two lines from the book as examples of memorable **dialogue**.

_____

_____

_____

7.   Summarise the **plot** of the book in one brief paragraph. (Hint: Name a key event from the beginning, middle and end.)

_____

_____

_____

_____

_____

_____

8.   Find your favourite **illustration** in the book. As you describe it, explain how this drawing works to aid the reader's imagination.

_____

_____

9.   State your opinion of the book's **title**. Does the title give a good clue as to what the story is about? Why or why not? Suggest a different title that would have worked as well.

_____

_____

_____

_____

10.   State two reasons why you *would* or *would not* recommend this novel to your readers.

_____

_____

_____

_____

ANSWERS

Words and meanings: Chapter 1 page 10

A. Across: 3. unforeseen 6. muscular 7. duties

   8. professor

   Down: 1. route 2. generous 3. usual

   4. features 5. brief

B. 1. unforeseen 2. duties 3. muscular

   4. brief 5. professor 6. generous

   7. usual 8. route 9. features

Recalling details: Chapter 1 page 11

   1. b 2. c 3. a 4. b 5. c 6. a 7. c 8. b 9. c

Synonyms and antonyms: Chapter 1 page 12

A.
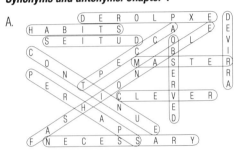

B. 1. perhaps 2. habits

   3. explored 4. observed

   5. duties 6. clever

   7. arrived 8. master

   9. necessary 10. accept

   11. continue 12. fashionable

C. Answers will vary. Possible answers:

   1. robber 2. short 3. rarely 4. stingy

Words and meanings: Chapter 2 page 13

A.
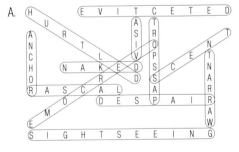

B. 1. fake 2. fail

   3. despised 4. deceitful

   5. agreed 6. shouted

   7. little 8. departed

C. 1. rascal 2. naked 3. scent 4. despair

Cause and effect: Chapter 2 page 14

A. 1. d 2. h 3. a 4. e 5. c 6. g 7. b 8. f

B. 1. Fix believes it is the stolen money.

   2. Mr Fix nearly jumps in surprise.

   3. They think his trip around the world is actually an escape.

Words and meanings: Chapter 3 page 15

A.
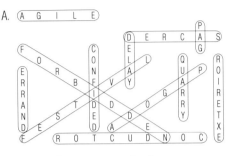

B. 1. pagoda 2. agile

   3. forbidden 4. conductor

   5. festival 6. quarry

   7. confided 8. gap

   9. sacred 10. errand

Sequence of events: Chapter 3 page 16

Sentence completion:

   1. transportation 2. sacrifice 3. gained 4. errand

   5. conductor 6. pagoda 7. rabbit 8. elephant

   9. curious 10. train 11. rescue 12. rajah

   13. priests

Sequence: 9, 12, 3, 2, 8, 5, 4, 10, 1, 7, 13, 11, 6

Words and meanings: Chapter 4 page 17

A. Across: 3. vowed 4. risky 6. stupor

   7. ghost 8. gratitude

   Down: 1. merchant 2. prisoners 5. orphan 9. icy

B. 1. merchant 2. stupor 3. gratitude 4. risky

   5. prisoners 6. icy 7. orphan 8. vowed 9. ghost

Comprehension check: Chapter 4 page 18

   1. c 2. b 3. c 4. b 5. c 6. a 7. b 8. a 9. c

Inference: Chapter 4 page 19

   1. The guide himself was Indian.

   2. They'd be harder to see under the cover of darkness.

   3. She wasn't safe in India and she had a cousin who lived in Hong Kong.

   4. Their first plan of rescue had failed.

   5. It was the custom to burn the wife of a dead rajah.

   6. They saw the supposedly dead rajah rise up and run off.

   7. A bullet whizzed through his hat as they ran away.

   8. She wept thankful tears.

Words and meanings: Chapter 5 — page 20

A. Across: 2. reward   6. satisfaction   7. fury   8. suspicions

Down: 1. bound   3. witnesses   4. reserve

5. intrude   6. spy

B. 1. reserve   2. suspicions, spy   3. witnesses   4. bound

5. reward   6. intrude   7. fury   8. satisfaction

Recalling details: Chapter 5 — page 21

1. b   2. a   3. c   4. c   5. b   6. a   7. b   8. a   9. c

Words and meanings: Chapter 6 — page 22

A.

B. 1. progress   2. pyramid

3. Acrobats   4. allies

5. typhoon   6. lobby

7. rumpled   8. hoist

Sequence of events: Chapter 6 — page 23

Sentence completion:

1. pyramid   2. calm   3. friends   4. Yokohama

5. Fogg   6. audience   7. typhoon   8. roof

9. San Francisco   10. neck   11. cannon   12. clown

13. servant

Sequence: 8, 3, 13, 5, 1, 10, 2, 9, 11, 12, 4, 6, 7

Character study: Chapter 6 — page 24

A. 1. generous, bold   2. secretive, determined

3. acrobatic, apologetic   4. grateful, enthusiastic

B. 1. Fogg   2. Mr Fix   3. Passepartout

4. Passepartout   5. Fogg

C. 1. John Bunsby   2. Mr Batulcar   3. John Bunsby

4. Mr Batulcar

Words and meanings: Chapter 7 — page 25

A. Across: 4. rapid   6. blockade   7. rally

Down: 1. budge   2. expected   3. buffalo

4. reverse   5. hubbub

B. 1. pistols   2. guard   3. hobby   4. problem   5. enraged

6. travellers

C. 1. b   2. d   3. a   4. c

Cause and effect: Chapter 7 — page 26

A. 1. f   2. g   3. c   4. a   5. b   6. d   7. h   8. e

B. 1. Both of them are knocked down.

2. Passepartout is furious at the delay.

3. To walk around it, passengers would first have to travel 16 kilometres.

Words and meanings: Chapter 8 — page 27

A.

B. 1. duel   2. insolent, diamond, spade

3. landmarks   4. unconscious

5. huddled   6. frank

7. throttle   8. Fort

Comprehension check: Chapter 8 — page 28

A. 1. F   2. T   3. T   4. F   5. F   6. T

7. F   8. T   9. T   10. T   11. F   12. F

B. Answers will vary. Possible answers:

1. Bound for New York, the train heads east.

2. The engineer's body pushes the throttle forward.

3. Passepartout separates the cars from the engines.

4. Passepartout is taken prisoner by the departing Sioux.

5. Fogg, Passepartout and Aouda continue their journey on a sled.

6. In Chicago, they catch the train bound for New York.

Words and meanings: Chapter 9 — page 29

A. Across: 1. capital   4. obstacles   7. wager

8. feats   9. greedy   10. masts

Down: 2. instant   3. persisted   5. bribed   6. cabins

B. 1. cabins, masts   2. capital   3. wager

4. greedy, instant   5. obstacles   6. feats

7. persisted, bribed

Comprehension check: Chapter 9 — page 30

1. steamer, Liverpool   2. docks, trading

3. captain, passengers   4. Captain Speedy, command

5. greedy, bribe   6. Newfoundland, *Henrietta*

7. engineer, Bordeaux   8. London, arrested

ANSWERS

Words and meanings: Chapter 10

A.

```
L U F H T I A F
T         R     S U S P E N S E   T
N   C A X       M   D   F           E
O   Y         E M R O     M         L
B   N     B       R U             E
L   O     O   W   A T     M         G
E   M     T U   T N               R
    E   A E G D U R   G           A
    C                 S             M
        L A N I M I R C             S
```

B. 1. telegrams   2. noble

    3. exact   4. bonds

    5. suspense   6. murmur

    7. ceremony   8. grudge

    9. faithful   10. eastward

Sequence of events: Chapter 10

Sentence completion:

    1. detective   2. cheering   3. forgiveness   4. bride

    5. gas   6. criminal   7. relatives   8. reward

    9. door   10. fortune   11. wife   12. Sunday

    13. ceremony

Sequence: 11, 10, 4, 13, 2, 1, 5, 9, 3, 12, 6, 8, 7

Personalising story events: Chapter 10

Answers will vary.

Book sequence

Sentence completion:

    1. *Carnatic*   2. *General Grant*   3. seconds   4. tour

    5. pagoda   6. Chicago   7. reconsider   8. rajah

    9. *Henrietta*   10. Bombay   11. San Francisco

    12. house   13. discovery

Sequence: 7, 8, 13, 2, 5, 10, 3, 6, 11, 4, 9, 1, 12

Final exam – 1

    1. d   2. c   3. b   4. a   5. d

Final exam – 2

1. He read it in a newspaper article.

2. He said that he had a sixth sense about such things.

3. A suttee is an ancient Indian ceremony in which a living wife is burned to death along with her husband's corpse.

4. Passepartout turned down Fix's offer to share the reward if Passepartout could keep Fogg from leaving Hong Kong.

5. The coal was running out and Fogg needed more fuel to reach Liverpool.

6. Fogg knocked him down with a single blow.

7. He saw Fogg holding Aouda's hand.

Beyond the text

Answers will vary.

Plot study

Answers will vary.

Theme analysis

Answers will vary.

Character study

Answers will vary.

Vocabulary study

Answers will vary.

Glossary study

Answers will vary.

Book review
pages 43–44

Answers will vary.

Prim-Ed Publishing www.prim-ed.com   Around the world in 80 days   47